STO

FRIENDS
OF ACPL

The Pedlar of Swaffham

The Pedlar

by Kevin Crossley-Holland

The Seabury Press · New York

# of Swaffham

illustrated by Margaret Gordon

Copyright © 1971 by Kevin Crossley-Holland and Margaret Gordon.
Library of Congress Catalog Card Number: 70-129208. Printed in Japan. All rights reserved.

CO. SCHOOLS
C781377

One night John Chapman had a dream.

A man stood by him, dressed in a surcoat as red as blood; and the man said, 'Go to London Bridge. Go and be quick. Go, good will come of it.'

John the pedlar woke with a start. 'Cateryne,' he whispered. 'Cateryne, wake up! I've had a dream.'

Cateryne, his wife, groaned and tossed and turned. 'What?' she said.

'I've had a dream.'

'Go to sleep, John,' she said; and she fell asleep again.

Then John lay and wondered at his dream; and while he lay wondering he too fell asleep. But the man in scarlet came a second time, and said, 'Go to London Bridge. Go and be quick. Go, good will come of it.'

The pedlar sat up in the dark. 'Cateryne!' he growled. 'Wake up! Wake up! I've had the same dream again.'

Cateryne groaned and tossed and turned. 'What?' she said.

Then John told her his dream.

'You,' she said, 'you would believe anything.'

The moment he woke next morning, the pedlar of Swaffham remembered his dream. He told it to his children, Margaret and Hue and Dominic. He told it to his wife again.

'Forget it!' said Cateryne.

So John went about his business and, as usual, his mastiff went with him. He fed his pig and hens in the back yard. He hoisted his pack on to his broad shoulders and went to the market place; he set up his stall of pots and pans, household goods of one kind and another, phials and potions, special trimmings for ladies' gowns. He gossiped with his friends—the butcher, the baker, the smith, the shoemaker, and the weaver, the dyer, and many another. But no matter what he did, the pedlar could not escape his dream. He shook his lion-head, he rubbed his blue eyes, but the dream seemed real and everything else seemed dreamlike. 'What am I to do?' he said.

And his mastiff opened his jaws, and yawned.

That evening John Chapman walked across the market place to the tumbledown church. And there he found the thin priest, Master Fuller; his holy cheekbones shone in the half-light. 'Well, what is it?' Master Fuller said.

Then John told him about his strange dream.

'I dream, you dream, everyone dreams,' said the priest impatiently, swatting dust from his black gown. 'It has no significance. If you must dream,' he added, 'dream of how we can get gold to rebuild our church. This ramshackle place is an insult to God.'

The two of them stood and stared sadly about them: all the walls of stone were rickety and uneven; the roof of the north aisle had fallen in, and through it they could see the crooked spire.

John Chapman sighed a long sigh. 'Gold,' he said. 'I wish I could.'

Then the pedlar left the church and went back to his small cottage. But he was still uneasy; his wide, friendly face wrinkled with thought. Nothing he did, and nothing anyone had said, seemed to make any difference; he could not forget his dream.

That night Cateryne said, 'You've talked and talked of the man with the surcoat as red as blood. You've been more dreaming than awake. Perhaps, perhaps after all you must go to London Bridge.'

'I'll go,' said John, 'I'll go and be quick.'

.Next day, John Chapman got up at first light. At once he began to make ready for his journey. 'I must take this,' he said, and he said,'I must take that.' He hurried about, he banged his head against a beam, his face turned red. 'I must take five gold pieces,' he said. 'I must take my cudgel.'

'You must take your hood,' said Cateryne.

Then John looked at his mastiff. 'I must take you,' he said.

And the mastiff thumped the ground with his tail; dust and chaff flew through the air.

'Tell no one where I've gone,' said John Chapman. 'I don't want to be the laughing-stock of Swaffham.'

Then, while the pedlar ate his fill of meat and curds, Cateryne put more food into his pack—cheese, and two loaves made of beans and bran, and a gourd full of ale.

So everything was ready. And just as the June sun rose behind clouds, a great coin of gold, John kissed his wife and his children good-bye.

'Come back,' called little Dominic.

They stood by the door, the four of them, waving and waving until the pedlar with his pack, his cudgel and mastiff, had walked out of Swaffham; out of sight.

John Chapman strode past the archery butts just outside the town; he hurried between fields white with sheep. At first he knew the way well, but then the rough highway that men called the Gold Road left the open fields behind and passed through sandy heathland where there were no people, no sheep, no villages.

Soon the rain came, heavy, blurring everything. John pulled his hood over his

head, but the water seeped through it. It soaked through his clothes, dripped from his nose.

By midday, he was tired and steaming. So he stopped to eat food and give a bone to his mastiff. And while they ate, some lord's messenger, decked out in red and blue, galloped by and spattered them with mud.

'The devil take him!' the pedlar said.

During the afternoon, the rain eased and the pedlar and his dog were able to quicken their pace. They made good progress; one by one the milestones fell away.

But that evening it grew dark before the pedlar could find any shelter, even a peasant's shack or some deserted hovel. John had no choice but to sleep in the open, under an oak tree. 'God help us,' he said, 'if there are wolves.'

But there were no wolves, only strange nightsounds: the tree groaning and creaking, wind in the moaning leaves and wind in the rustling grass, the barking of fox and vixen. When first light came, John could barely get to his feet for the ache in his cold bones and the cramp in his empty stomach.

And his mastiff hobbled about as if he were a hundred.

So for four days they walked on. Every hour contained its own surprise; John talked to a friendly priest who had been to Jerusalem; he walked with a couple of vagabonds who wanted him to go to a fair at Waltham; he shook off a rascally pardoner who tried to sell him a ticket to heaven; he saw rabbits, and hares, and deer; he gazed down from hill-crests at tapestries of fields; he followed the way through dark forests where only silence lived. Never in his life had John met so many strangers nor set eyes on so many strange things. He said to his mastiff, 'We're foreigners in our own country.'

Sometimes the pedlar's pack chafed at his shoulders; often he envied the many travellers with horses—pilgrims and merchants, scholars and monks; but not for one moment did he forget his purpose. For as long as it was light, John Chapman made haste, following the Gold Road south towards London. And each night, after the first, he stayed at a wayside inn or in a monastery.

On the morning of the fifth day, the pedlar and his dog came at last to the City of London. At the sight of the high walls, the pedlar's heart quickened, and so did his step.

And his mastiff leaped about, barking for excitement.

They hurried through the great gate; and there before them were crowds of people coming and going, to-ing and fro-ing; men shouting their wares; women jostling, talking; small children begging; and many, many others sitting in rags in the filthy street. And there were houses to left and right; and after that, more houses, more streets, and always more people. John had never seen such a sight nor smelt such a stink nor heard such a hubbub.

A tide of people swept him along until he came to a place where four ways met. There, John stopped a man with a lop-sided face and a stoop, and asked him the way to London Bridge.

'Straight on.' said the man. 'Straight as an arrow's flight, all the way.'

The broad river gleamed under the sun, silver and green, ruckled by wind; gulls
swooped and climbed again, shrieking. The great bridge spanned the water, the long

bridge with its houses overhanging the river. It was a sight to gladden any man. And when he saw it, John Chapman got to his knees. He thanked God that his journey had been safe, and that he had come at last to London Bridge.

But the moment the pedlar stepped on to the bridge itself he felt strangely foolish. All his hope and his excitement seemed long ago. People were passing this way and that, but no one looked at John. No one took the least notice of him. Having at last found London Bridge, the poor pedlar of Swaffham felt utterly lost.

He walked up and down; he stared about him; he counted the houses, then recounted them; he watched boats shoot the bridge; he added up his money. Hour after hour after hour went by; the pedlar waited.

Late that afternoon, a group of pilgrims, all with horses, gathered on the Bridge. And they began to sing: *As you came from the holy-land of Walsingham* . . .

'Walsingham!' cried John. 'I know it well. I've taken my wares there a hundred times. What does this song mean? Will *this* explain my dream?'

As if to answer him, the group of pilgrims broke up and rode off, still singing, even as he hurried towards them.

'Wait!' bawled John. 'Wait!'

But the hooves of the horses clattered, they struck sparks from the cobbles. And the poor pedlar was left, in the fading light, looking after them.

He felt heavy-hearted. He knew there was nothing he could do until the next morning. He wearily asked of a passer-by where he might stay, and was directed to

The Three Cranes, a hostelry on the riverside, a stopping-place for passengers coming down the river, a sleeping-place for travellers in all weathers.

There John Chapman and his mastiff shared a bed of straw; they were tired out, dog-tired.

Early on the morning of the second day the pedlar and his dog returned to the bridge. Once again, hour after hour after hour went by. John felt foolish, then lonely, then hopeless, then angry.

Late that day he saw a man with matted red hair lead on to the bridge a loping black bear. 'Look!' he exclaimed delightedly.

And his mastiff looked, carefully.

'A rare sight!' said John. 'A sight worth travelling miles to see. Perhaps *this* is what I have travelled for. Perhaps here I shall find the meaning of my dream.' And the pedlar greeted the man; he thought he had never seen anyone so ugly in all his life. 'Does the bear dance?' he asked.

'He does,' said the man. He squinted at John. 'Give me gold and I'll show you.'

'Another time,' said the pedlar. He stooped to pat the bear's gleaming fur.

'Leave him alone!' snapped the man.

'Why?' asked John.

'He'll have your hand off, that's why.'

The pedlar stepped back hastily; he called his mastiff to heel.

'He had a hand off at Cambridge,' said the man. 'So you watch it! Hands off!'

'Hardly a pleasant travelling companion,' said John.

'Mind your words,' growled the man, and squinted more fiercely than ever. 'He'll bite your head off.'

'Like you,' said John. And with that he walked away.

So the second day turned out no better than the first. And on the third day the poor pedlar waited and waited, he walked up and down and he walked to and fro, and no good came of it. 'Now we have only one piece of gold left,' he said to his mastiff. 'Tomorrow we'll have to go home; I'm a great fool to have come at all.'

And the mastiff groaned.

At that moment a man shaped like an egg waddled towards John, and greeted him. 'For three days,' he said, 'you've loitered on this bridge.'

'How do you know?' asked John, surprised.

'I know,' said the man mysteriously.

'How?' repeated John.

'I keep a shop here and I've seen you come and go, come and go from dawn to dusk.' He narrowed his eyes. 'What are you up to? What are you waiting for?'

'That's exactly what I was asking myself,' said the pedlar sadly. 'To tell you the truth, I've walked to London Bridge because I dreamed that good would come of it.'

'Lord preserve me!' exclaimed the shopkeeper. 'What a waste of time!'

John Chapman threw back his head and sighed; he didn't know what to say.

'Only fools follow dreams,' said the shopkeeper. 'Why, last night I dreamed that a pot of gold lay buried by a hawthorn tree in a garden; and the garden belonged to

some pedlar, in a place called Swaffham.'

'A pot of gold?' said John. 'A pedlar?'

'You see?' said the egg-shaped man. 'Nonsense.'

'Yes,' said John.

'Dreams are just dreams,' said the shopkeeper with a wave of his pudgy hand.
'You're wasting your time. Take my advice and go back home.'

'I will,' said John Chapman.

So it was that, in the evening of the twelfth day after his departure, John Chapman and his dog—spattered with mud, aching and blistered, weary but excited—returned home. They saw the leaning church spire; they passed the archery butts; they came at last to John's small cottage of wattle and daub.

Cateryne had never in her life been so glad to see her husband. Margaret and Hue leaped about; their ashen hair danced on their heads. 'Come back!' cried little Dominic.

'So,' asked Cateryne softly, 'what of the dream, John?'

Then John told them in his own unhurried way. He told them of his journey;

he told them of the long days on London Bridge; and, at last, he told them of the shopkeeper's words.

'A man follows a dream, and returns with another man's dream,' said Cateryne. 'That's very strange. And how can it be true?'

'I've asked myself that a thousand times,' the pedlar said, 'and there's only one way to find out.'

The gnarled hawthorn tree stood at the end of the yard; it had lived long, perhaps hundreds of years. And its leaves seemed now to whisper secrets.

The hens clucked in the dusk; and the pig lay still, one eye open, watching John.

'I'll start here,' said the pedlar quietly. Then he gripped his round-edged spade and began to dig, firmly, rhythmically, making a mound of the loose earth. Beads of sweat trickled down his broad face, and he stopped to strip off his surcoat.

'Can I?' asked Margaret. 'Let me!' said Hue.

'No!' said John. 'Wait!' And again he dug, firmly, rhythmically. The gleaming spade bit into the packed soil.

At once they heard it, they all heard it together, the grind of metal against metal, muted by soil. The pedlar took one look at his family and began to dig as fast as he could.

Earth flew through the air; the pedlar gasped. 'Look!' he said breathlessly. 'Look! Look!'

He had partly uncovered a great metal pot.

John tossed away his spade. He bent down and tugged. He worked his fingers further under the pot and tugged again. Then suddenly the dark earth gave up its secret; John staggered away, grasping the pot. As he fell backwards, the lid flew off. Coins rained on the pedlar's face; the ground was carpeted with gold.

They were all utterly silent, dumbfounded. Only the tree, the tree in the gloom went on whispering.

'John, John, what shall we do with it?' said Cateryne.

'First,' said the pedlar, slapping earth and straw from his surcoat with his great hands, 'we must gather it quickly and take it inside.'

So they picked up the gold coins and put them back into the pot, and together carried it into their cottage. They placed it on the floor, in front of the fire.

'Look! What's this?' said Hue, lifting the lid off the pot, and rubbing it. 'It's writing.'

John took the lid from him and frowned over it. 'Yes,' he said slowly. 'It's words.' He smiled shrewdly. 'I'll hide the gold here,' he said, 'and take the empty pot with the rest of my wares to the market place. Someone is sure to come along and read it for us.'

Next morning the pedlar was early in the market place, standing over his wares with his elder children and his dog. In no time Master Fuller came picking his way towards them through the higgledy-piggledy stalls—a dark figure amongst bright colours, a silent man in a sea of noise. 'John Chapman,' he exclaimed. 'Where have you been?'

'To and fro,' said the pedlar. 'To and fro.'

'And where were you last Sunday?' asked the priest. 'I missed you at Mass.'

'Well, I . . . .'

'Excuses! Always excuses!' said the priest sharply. 'Who shall be saved? Men are empty vessels.' And he rapped the great metal pot with his knuckles; it rang with a fine deep note. 'Now that's a fine vessel,' said Master Fuller.

'It is,' agreed John Chapman.

'There are words on it,' said the priest. He raised the lid and narrowed his eyes.

The pedlar looked at him anxiously ; Margaret and Hue stood petrified.

'It's in Latin,' said Master Fuller. 'It says, *Under me* . . . yes . . . *Under me there lies another richer than I.*' The priest frowned. 'What can that mean?' he asked.

John Chapman scratched the back of his head; his heart pounded so loudly he thought the priest would be able to hear it.

'Where did you get it?'

'Out of a back yard,' the pedlar said, shrugging his broad shoulders.

'I must go,' said the priest suddenly. 'All this idle chatter. Men would do better to give time to God.' And leaving, as ever, a pointed remark behind him, the priest walked off towards the rickety church.

As soon as his back was turned, the pedlar packed up his wares and, led by his children, followed by his mastiff, he hurried home.

'This time you shall dig,' the pedlar told his children.

Then Hue grasped the spade and began to dig; the rounded edge sheared through the darkness. His face soon flushed; he began to pant.

'Now let Margaret have it,' the pedlar said.

Hue scowled, and handed the spade to his sister.

Then Margaret threw back her hair and stepped into the pit, and dug yet deeper. Everyone watched her. Deeper and deeper. Then, once again, metal grated against metal—the same unmistakable sound. Margaret shivered with excitement. 'You,' she said, and handed the spade back to her father.

Once more John dug as fast as he could; once more he tugged and tugged; and once more the reluctant earth yielded its secret—a second great pot, an enormous pot twice as large as the first. The pedlar could barely heave it out of the hole and on to the level ground.

When he levered off the lid, they all saw that this pot too was heaped to the brim with glowing gold. 'It's like a dream,' said John, 'and because of a dream. But we're awake, and rich.'

Cateryne stared into the gaping, black hole. 'Who could have hidden it there?' she said. 'And why?'

'How shall we ever know?' replied the pedlar. 'Someone who once lived here? Travellers on the Gold Road? How can we tell? Perhaps we're not even meant to tell. After all, men say the hawthorn is a magic tree.'

'What are we going to do with it?' asked Cateryne.

For a moment John did not reply. His blue eyes closed, his face wrinkled. 'I know,' he said at last. 'I know.' And his face lit up with a slow smile. 'A little we'll keep—enough to pay for our own small needs this year and every year, enough to buy ourselves a strip of land. But all the rest, every coin, we must give to Master Fuller to build the new church.'

Cateryne drew in her breath and smiled and clapped her hands. 'Amen!' she said. 'Amen!' chimed the children.

'In this way,' said John, 'everyone in Swaffham will share in the treasure.'

'Now,' said Cateryne, 'and in time to come.'

That afternoon, John Chapman found the priest skulking in the gloom of the tumbledown church. 'Master Fuller,' he said, 'I would like to give gold for the new church.'

'Every piece counts,' said the priest.

'I have many,' said John.

'Many?' said the priest suspiciously.

'Wait here,' said the pedlar. And he hurried out of the church and back to his cottage. There, he counted one hundred pieces of gold for his own needs and the needs of his family, and hid them in the inner room, under the bed of straw.

Then the pedlar and his wife, and Margaret and Hue, followed by Dominic and their loyal mastiff, carried the hoard to Swaffham Church. As they crossed the market place, they shouted to their friends, 'Come with us! Come to the church!'

So the butcher, the baker, the smith, the shoemaker, and the weaver, the dyer and many another left their work. And in no time, a great procession, curious and chattering, was filing into the silent church.

In the nave, John and Cateryne turned their pot upside down. Margaret and Hue did the same. A mound of gold coins glowed mysteriously in the half-light.

The townspeople gasped, and stared at it, silent with awe.

Master Fuller's bony face cracked into a grin; his eyes gleamed. 'Explain!' he said.

So John Chapman told them the whole story, this story, from beginning to end. And no storyteller, before or since, has had such an audience.

Then the priest rubbed his hands. 'There's enough gold here,' he said, 'to rebuild the north aisle, and the steeple.'

The townsfolk began to whisper excitedly.

Then the priest raised his hand, and he said, 'Let us pray, and, after that. . . . let us sing and dance the night away.'

'Sing in the churchyard? Dance in the churchyard?' everyone cried.

'Even until this old church falls down,' said Master Fuller. And for the first time that anyone could remember, he laughed. He threw back his head and laughed.

CO. SCHOOLS
C781377

So, that same evening, a man with a bugle and a man with a humstrum and a man with cymbals and clappers played as if they meant to raise the roof off every house in Swaffham; the townsfolk sang and danced until midnight. And John the dreamer was tossed by the dancers into the air, higher and higher, towards the stars.

And his mastiff sat on his haunches, and laughed.

So Swaffham Church was rebuilt, and it owed more to the generosity of John Chapman than any other man. In the year 1462, the pedlar (or chapman) paid for the new north aisle and contributed to the cost of the spire. This is recorded in the 15th century Black Book *which is still in Swaffham Church Library, and which includes a list of benefactors of the church.*

In the aisle, John Chapman had his own chair—perhaps the only chair in the church—carved with the figure of a pedlar with a pack on his back and a mastiff at his side. And the aisle's windows contained pictures of the pedlar with his wife and three children.

The rebuilding of the church was actually begun in 1454. It was not completed until the middle of the 16th century; but this time it was built to last. You can see it today. You can see fragments of John Chapman's chair and of the old stained glass. You can see the spire, a pointed reminder, from miles off.

GLOSSARY

Archery Butts A mark or target for archery practice. By law every male peasant had to possess longbow and arrows and practise regularly at the butts.

Chapman A pedlar. People were often called by their professions, for instance Butcher, Cooper, Taylor, Smith.

Clappers Castanets.

The Gold Road It ran from Lynn, a major port in Norfolk, to London, and was so called because of the many valuable exports and imports carried along it.

Humstrum A one-stringed roughly-made musical instrument.

Mastiff A powerful dog with a large head, drooping ears and pendulous lips.

Pardoner A man authorised by the Pope to forgive sins in return for money. As often as not they were rascals, and thieved from the poor.

Shoot the Bridge The water passed very swiftly under London Bridge. So boats 'shot the bridge' as, today, boats 'shoot the falls'.

The Three Cranes A hostelry in Upper Thames Street. Passengers landed here and rejoined their boat at Billingsgate (or vice versa) for fear of an upset in the turbulent water under the bridge.

Wattle and daub Rods or stakes, interlaced with twigs, used to make a framework for walls. This was covered with daub which was a brittle plaster made of a mixture of dung and mud and straw.